Emerald Shadow

Steampunk OZ: Book 3

by Steve DeWinter

Summary

There is no yellow brick road here. No emerald city. No lollipop guild. This is the Australis Penal Colony, a continent sized prison referred to the world over as the Outcast Zone. Built to contain the world's most dangerous criminals, OZ ended up the dumping ground for everything polite society deemed undesirable.

Book 3

Having survived Nero's gladiator arena, Dorothy and her new group of friends are on the run and face danger at every turn.

This book is a work of fiction. References to real people, events, establishments, organization, or locales are intended only to provide a sense of authenticity, and are used fictitiously. All other characters, and all incidents and dialogue, are drawn from the author's imagination and are not to be construed as real.

Ramblin' Prose Publishing
Copyright © 2014 Steve DeWinter
All rights reserved. Used under authorization.
www.stevedw.com

eBook Edition
ISBN-10: 1-61978-036-4
ISBN-13: 978-1-61978-036-1

Paperback Edition
ISBN-10: 1-61978-037-2
ISBN-13: 978-1-61978-037-8

Chapter 1

Amanda pressed the spyglass to her eye and focused on the small group as they made their way through the back alleys of the city.

She struggled to keep them in view and lost sight of them several times as the gondola rocked back and forth from being pushed around by the heavy air currents above Roma. She slammed her hand on the wood paneling that bordered the windows on the bridge of her airship. "Keep the ship steady."

The helmsman cringed at her outburst. "Yes ma'am."

She refocused the spyglass and watched as, yet again, Nero's men almost stumbled upon the small group before turning the wrong way and completely missing them.

She was glad that this ongoing comedy of errors kept the small band of misfits from being captured.

Nero had his chance to turn over the East Marshal. Not only had he failed to do that, but he let her escape. It would have been comical if it were not for the fact that she had escaped with the one thing her mother needed to become Queen over all of OZ.

Well, maybe not all of OZ.

The Southern Marshal had built a wall that cut off her territory from the rest of the continent.

Her mother would still be Queen over the parts of OZ that really mattered. Once she was Queen, she could knock down that wall and conquer the Southern Territories if she so desired.

For now, the Southern Territories did not matter.

The small group turned west down an alley and started moving away from her. Without taking her eye off the spyglass she barked commands at her helmsman.

"Turn thirty degrees to the port and increase speed to slow ahead."

"Aye, aye captain," the helmsman responded and spun the ship's wheel. He grabbed the handle on the bridge's engine order telegraph and shifted the dial to the section marked "Slow Ahead".

She felt the vibrations in the floor shift as the steam turbines in the engine room spun the external propellers faster.

Her airship was built using the latest scientific theories, both inside and outside of OZ, in aerodynamics and propulsion.

She commanded the fastest airship in all of OZ.

Nobody was getting away from her.

Caleb stepped out of the kitchen door to the back alley where Dorothy, Jasper and the two automatons waited.

"The innkeeper says we can stay for a few days and promises to keep mum that we're here."

Jasper plucked at his bottom lip. A nervous habit Dorothy had noticed he exhibited during the short time she knew him.

She felt just as nervous about being discovered. "How do you know he'll keep his word?"

Caleb looked at her. "Because I paid him more then he asked for."

"Does he have somewhere to keep the Woodsman?" She asked.

He shook his head. "No. But I know of an old barn just outside of town where we can hide him."

"I don't like splitting us up."

"I know, but we don't have any other choice."

She looked deep into Caleb's eyes. "How safe are we here?"

He gripped her shoulders and squeezed them lightly, trying to reassure her. "Very safe."

Amanda watched the group break into the barn outside of town and leave behind the Woodsman. She followed their journey back to the inn through the spyglass. Ten minutes after they disappeared inside, her spy on the ground transmitted a message to her by heliograph, a small mirror that reflected sunlight for communicating over vast distances.

The group had retired to their room and ordered dinner. They obviously planned to stay there much longer than she was going to allow them. That also meant she had little bit of time before she had to collect them.

She refocused her attention on the dilapidated barn.

Woodsmen were plentiful in the Eastern Territories, but they just didn't have very many of them in the West. If she returned with a newly refurbished Woodsman, along with the East Marshal star, her mother would be proud of her. So proud she might even give her some territory to rule over.

"Take the ship to ground. Inform the men we are going to be loading on some cargo."

The helmsmen snapped to attention. "Yes ma'am."

As Dorothy scooped boiled vegetables on to her plate, she noticed Scarecrow studying himself in a wall-mounted mirror. He traced the shallow dents on the side of his head with a finger before he turned to look at her. "What happened to my face?"

Dorothy laughed. "It was very heroic. You single-handedly destroyed the wireless radio controlling the Woodsman. "

Jasper spoke through mouthfuls of bread and gravy. "More like single-headedly."

If an automaton could look confused, Dorothy thought, Scarecrow sure looked it now. She suddenly remembered he was lying in pieces during the entire battle in the coliseum.

"While you were shut down, the Woodsman was trying to kill us."

Scarecrow stiffened as if in shock.

Dorothy could tell she wasn't explaining it very well. "Nero had a control device installed on the Woodsman's back. He was completely under Nero's control until Caleb used your head to smash it. Once destroyed, the Woodsman was able to follow my orders again."

Scarecrow turned to Caleb. "Couldn't you find something else to hit it with?"

Caleb tore a piece of meat from the roasted chicken with his fingers and popped it into his mouth with a smile. "It was the hardest thing I could find."

Jasper was laughing gravy out of his mouth. "Yeah well…"

There was a thump from the ceiling above them as if something very heavy just dropped onto the roof.

Everyone went silent and looked up.

Captain Stiles, the squad leader for Amanda's soldiers, watched as the last of his men slid down the rope that dangled from the airship and landed on the roof of the inn. He did not look at Amanda as he spoke. "I urge you to reconsider waiting until reinforcements arrive."

Amanda stood stock-still and gave him a hard stare back. "If we move now, we can take them by surprise. I will not make the same mistakes Nero made and let them get away."

Captain Stiles stood his ground. How could he expect a politician's spoiled little child to understand matters of war? "I wouldn't be saying this if we hadn't already lost five men trying to secure the Woodsman."

Amanda narrowed her eyes. "Are you questioning my judgment, Captain?"

He lowered his head. Whether or not she understood anything at all about strategy or tactics, she could still toss him and his family into the deepest dungeon for disobeying orders. "No ma'am."

"Good. Then proceed as planned."

"Yes ma'am."

"Let me know as soon as you have them and I will bring the airship back down."

"Yes ma'am."

Captain Stiles grabbed the rope and disappeared out the gondola door. As he slid down the rope, he wondered which god he had angered that put him under the command of such an inept child.

His boots landed on the roof and, as soon as he let go of the rope, the airship pulled away from the inn.

He retrieved his .44 caliber repeating Winchester carbine from the sling around his back and looked at his men. He shook his head and wondered if he should have stood up to the West Marshal's daughter sooner.

Having only four men left, including himself, it was going to be much more difficult to capture the fugitives. Especially, since one of the fugitives was an automaton.

Fortunately, his men were armed and, according to all intelligence reports, the fugitives were not. As long as he could get the fugitives together in a small group, he could keep them under control.

This might not be too bad, he thought. The element of surprise was always one of the better weapons he had at his disposal.

He pointed to the south end of the roof line. "Charlie, Edward. You secure the back entrance."

They both nodded their heads and rushed across the roof.

He looked at the youngest soldier he had ever commanded in OZ. The boy could not have been more than 16 years old. He usually did not recruit young boys from the general populace for security detail, but the West Marshal had been gearing up for an invasion of the Northern Territory's as part of her campaign to control all of OZ and she had taken all the older and stronger men for her vast army. Once they had control over the Eastern Territories, he would rebuild the Royal Security Forces with more able-bodied men, and not the children that he was forced to deal with now.

He nodded to the young kid who gripped his Winchester carbine more like a club than a rifle. He made a mental note to petition the West Marshal for better training of her soldiers.

"Cole, you're with me."

He thought he heard Cole's voice crack a little when he replied with a, "Yes sir!"

They ran along the roof to the north end of the inn and stopped. He looked over just in time to see the fugitives jump from the balcony of their room to the roof of an adjacent building. The girl was the last jump across and when she hit the roof, she turned around and looked up at him. There did not appear to be any fear her in her eyes, just a determination to get away. She spun back around and ran along the roof, following the rest of her party.

So much for the element of surprise.

He glanced back and yelled to get the attention of his men standing at the far end of the roof.

He pointed down as he yelled, "They jumped over to another building." The two men instantly began running back.

He spun back around and pointed to the roof below them. "Follow them."

Cole backed away from the edge of the roof, shaking his head. "No way. It's too far."

The fear he had hoped to see in the eyes of his quarry was instead deep set in the eyes of his soldier. He grabbed Cole's collar with both hands and nearly lifted him off his feet. "Either you jump or I throw you across."

The boy was practically in tears. "Okay, I'll jump."

He let go of him. "Just do what I do."

He took a few steps backward and then ran toward the edge of the roof. He launched himself off his feet and sailed across the open gap between the two buildings. He landed on the roof allowing his momentum to propel him into a somersault and back onto his feet in a crouch.

He stood up, straightened his coat and motioned for the boy to follow him.

Cole took a couple steps back before he ran for the edge of the roof. At the last moment, he faltered and ran off the edge of the roof rather than jumping off the roof.

Without the upward momentum provided by jumping off the roof, Cole dropped like a rock and disappeared below the roof line with a bloodcurdling scream that ended abruptly. The other two men ignored the death of Cole and vaulted from the inn to the other building without even slowing down.

They joined him as he ran across the rooftops, leaping from building to building in hot pursuit of his prey.

He was down to three men, including himself, and had lost the element of surprise. He needed to somehow even those odds. He glanced over his shoulder at the airship as it followed them across the rooftops. The fugitives had to know there was no way they could outrun the airship. Even though the only people on board the airship were Amanda, the helmsman and an engineer, all he had to do was make them think it was filled with soldiers and they would give up without a fight.

Despite slipping occasionally on the loose shingles of poorly maintained roofs, he ran as fast as he could and gained on them.

As he ran, he called out, "There's nowhere to go. Surrender now and I guarantee none of my soldiers will harm you."

The girl, the boy, the animal-man thing and the automaton kept running. His threats only seemed to make them run that much faster and they gave no indication that they planned to stop.

Since it was obvious they would not stop willingly, he had to give them another reason to stop.

He skidded to a halt on the roof and bent on one knee as he sighted down the barrel of his Remington carbine. The group ran away from him in a straight line, making it easy to target the automaton.

He held his breath to steady the rifle and squeezed the trigger.

The bullet whistled through the air and slammed into the back of the automaton, sending it pinwheeling off the edge of the roof.

The girl stopped running and screamed, "Scarecrow!"

The rest of the group stopped with her. They appeared to be having an argument that stopped when they noticed his men approaching them with rifles drawn. It was at that point that they raised their hands in defeat.

He vaulted over the gap between buildings and landed on the roof. He slung his Winchester behind his back to send the message to them that, not only were they his prisoner, he was not worried about them trying to escape again.

He looked at the ragtag group and wondered why the West Marshal was willing to risk so many lives to capture these people?

His focus turned to the man-beast. There weren't many of these around, and he thought he recognized this one.

"Aren't you Nero's personal bodyguard?"

The man-beast's fur bristled when he spoke. "Ex-bodyguard."

"So what did you do to fall out of favor with Nero?"

"I was repaying an old debt."

That wasn't the answer he had expected. Well, he thought, it hardly mattered. As long as the West Marshal wanted these people brought to her alive, that is exactly what he would do.

He waved a hand in the air.

Above them, the airship descended to collect them.

Captain Stiles smiled to himself as he watched the fear grow in his captives' faces. When the ship was only 20 feet above them, the man-beast suddenly leapt into the air and grabbed one of the tether ropes that hung along the side of the airship's gas envelope. He swung around on the rope and knocked Edward off the roof while, at the same time, the young boy and girl tackled Charlie.

As he grabbed for the rifle slung over his shoulder, the man-beast shoved him down from behind and ripped the Winchester carbine out of his grip.

He went from being in control of the situation to being a hostage within half a second. In addition, it had all taken place in the blind spot directly under the airship.

The man-beast jabbed the rifle barrel into the side of his jaw. "How many more men are aboard?"

"I have a heavily armed compliment of twenty men who will kill you where you stand unless you drop the rifle now."

The young boy he twisted Charlie's arm up behind his back. "Is he telling the truth?"

Through gritted teeth Charlie responded, "He's telling the truth"

The boy looked from Charlie back to him and squinted his eyes. He grabbed Charlie's hand and bent the pinky finger back until it snapped.

Charlie screamed, "It's just us. It's just us. There's nobody else."

The boy obviously did not trust Charlie was giving enough information. He grabbed the next finger and started pulling it back. "Then who's flying the ship?"

Captain Stiles had to get the situation back under control and keep Charlie from talking. "That's enough…" But he was cut off by a sharp pain to the back of his head and everything went black.

It did not feel like any time had passed before someone was slapping him awake. His eyes snapped open and he looked up at Amanda, who stood over him looking down. He could still tell he was up on the roof and the sun had not traveled very far since he had been knocked out.

He squinted up and Amanda. "What happened?"

"You handed them my ship," Amanda said.

Chapter 2

The gondola of the airship swayed lightly in a rhythmic pattern and kept Dorothy focused while she repaired the Woodsman. Jasper found him in the cargo hold after they gained control of the airship.

She wiped her hands on an oily cloth as she regarded the Woodsman with a smile. "That should do it."

Jasper took the filthy rag from her and tossed it in the corner of the cargo area of the airship. "How do you think he got aboard?"

She shrugged her shoulders. "They must've been watching us the whole time and took him from the barn right after we left."

Jasper ran a hand over the fresh dents and scratches in the Woodsman's armor plating. "Looks like he put up quite a fight."

She pointed to the burn mark to one side. "At least until they zapped him with that electric prod."

Jasper's hand reached to the side of his stomach. "Yeah, I didn't like that thing either."

She stared down at the pile of Scarecrow parts. It was probably best to leave the automatons shut off until they landed.

Working on the Woodsman had taken her mind off the situation she was in. As she walked out of the cargo hold, her mind raced with how bad things had gotten in the past few days.

If someone asked her what she had done with her life she never thought she could say she was a runaway, a stowaway, a killer, a thief, a fugitive, and now a hijacker.

Why was it so easy to commit crime in OZ?

Could she have avoided any of it?

As she stepped onto the bridge of the airship, Caleb leaned on the ship's wheel and pointed out the windows to the faintly illuminated eastern sky.

"The sun will be up soon and they'll be looking for this ship. We better land and continue the rest of the way on foot."

She looked at Caleb and saw the same level of weariness that must've been evident on her own face.

"How long do you think we have before she catches up to us?"

"If we can get some new clothes we might be able to keep from getting discovered until we're safe inside Center City."

"What makes you think Center City will be any safer than out here?"

He shrugged his shoulders. "It will be safe from any of the other marshals. And Amanda."

"I don't have any money for new clothes."

Caleb turned the wheel slightly and redirected the airship toward a blinking light on the horizon. "I guess we'll have to steal something once we make it to that town."

She looked out the window and saw her own weary face reflected back in the pane of glass. "That's just great."

The perspective of her face floating like a specter over the skyline of a small city in the distance seemed all too fitting. It was as if she cast a shadow over all of OZ just by being here.

Jasper appeared at the door to the bridge. "I felt the ship turn."

Dorothy continued to look out the window at their destination. "Caleb says we have to ditch the ship before we get caught."

Caleb nodded his head. "There's only one airship like this in all of OZ. As long as we are anywhere near it, we've got problems."

Jasper pointed out the window. "We're not going there, are we?"

Caleb twisted the wheel slightly. The airship pointed directly at the blinking light in the center of the city's skyline. "We have to get somewhere before the sun comes up and everybody can see us."

Jasper stared out the window. "We can't go there."

Dorothy turned to Jasper. "Why not?"

Jasper's mouth open and closed a few times as if he was unsure of what to say. He finally said, "We just can't. There's another town 20 miles to the west. If we fly low, no one will see us."

Caleb looked at him, his furry forehead wrinkled in confusion. "What's wrong with that town?"

Jasper still stared out the window. "Nothing specific. But I've heard rumors."

Dorothy and Caleb waited for him to finish, but when he didn't, Caleb spoke up. "I don't know what you heard, but we don't really have a choice." He tapped one of the dials in front of the ship's wheel with his finger. "We don't have enough fuel to make it anywhere else. We have to land here."

Dorothy glanced out at the growing skyline as they neared the city and then turned back to face Caleb and Jasper.

"You are both right. We don't have enough fuel to make it to the next town but we can't land this ship inside the city limits of any town or we'll have more trouble than we can handle."

Caleb looked even more confused than before. "What are you trying to say?"

"Just land us in that open field over there and we'll figure out another way to get to Center City without going through that town. Does that work for both of you?"

Jasper nodded his head.

Caleb only responded by twisting the ships' wheel and guiding the airship toward the field.

Jasper mumbled something about getting the Woodsman and Scarecrow ready and headed for the cargo bay.

Caleb remained silent as he lowered the airship effortlessly toward the field.

The bump of hitting the ground softly pulled her out of her dark thoughts and back to where she was right now. She looked over at Caleb. "Let's get going before someone spots us."

He grinned. "No argument from me there."

They climbed down the ladder to the cargo bay just as Jasper fired up the Woodsman. Scarecrow was already at the controls to lower the cargo bay door.

She looked at Jasper but pointed to Scarecrow. "Does he know how to work the bay doors?"

Jasper was guiding the Woodsman toward the door. "I showed him how."

"It feels like you're rushing us Jasper."

He looked at her, a worried expression on his face. "I just think we should get away from this airship as quickly as possible."

Caleb hopped down from the ladder behind her. "Are you sure that's all there is to it?"

Jasper didn't respond, but instead motioned toward Scarecrow.

Dorothy nodded to him and he pulled down on the lever. Jasper was on the door as soon as it was level with the cargo platform. "We have to go now before…" He was suddenly cut off by the sound of several cocking levers being pulled back on flintlock rifles.

The cargo door continued to swivel down to the ground and revealed several farmers pointing rifles up into the cargo bay.

One of the men pointing a flintlock rifle at them smiled when his eyes fell on Jasper. "Jasper?"

Dorothy glanced sideways at Jasper. "You know these people?"

Jasper never took his eyes off of the barrel pointed straight at him. "Sort of."

The man lowered his rifle. "Jasper Hawksley, Jr.?"

Jasper slightly waved a hand. "Um, hey. How you guys doing?"

"Don't you remember what we said would happen if you ever came back?"

Chapter 3

Dorothy found herself staring out through the bars of yet another cage. It surprised her how many prisons there were inside the world's largest prison.

Since coming to OZ, she has been inside a walled up city with no gate to the outside world, in a cage in the underground caverns below a coliseum and now she was in a cage inside of a barn. It was as if the only thing these people knew how to do was put each other in successively smaller cages.

Why did they even have cages inside a barn?

She glanced to one side and saw Caleb and Jasper both in cages of their own along the same wall of the barn as her cage.

She hollered over to Jasper. "What did you do to these guys?"

"Technically, I didn't do anything," he replied.

Caleb stood up in his cage and joined the conversation. "Then what are we doing in here?"

"It's kind of something my dad did."

One of the farmers, who had been relegated to guard duty, stepped into the barn. "No talking."

Dorothy called out to him. "I'm the East Marshal; you can't treat me like this."

The farmer sauntered up to her, his flintlock rifle resting casually on his shoulder. "You're not in the Eastern Territories anymore ma'am. You're within the borders of Center City. You ain't nobody here."

She slid down the bars and back into a sitting position on the straw covered floor. "So everyone keeps telling me."

She sat with her back against the bars of her cage and drew circles in the loose dirt. Her mind feverishly tried to formulate some plan of escape.

She was at a complete loss and if the guard kept them all from talking, she couldn't ask Caleb or Jasper for their input.

It felt like she had been sitting there for days, but it could not have been more than a couple of hours when a new guard came in and relieved the current guard.

This new guard watched her just as intently as the previous one, so talking to Caleb or Jasper was still out of the question. Nothing in her life before had prepared her for something like this. She hadn't known what to expect when she snuck on board William's airship, but it certainly wasn't this.

"Attention!" the guard yelled and startled her.

"All rise for Captain Myers."

The same man who identified Jasper when they first landed walked right up to her cage.

"My guard tells me that you claim to be the East Marshal?"

Dorothy stood a little straighter, hoping to portray some form of authority. "Yes, and I demand that you release us at once."

Captain Myers laughed. "Prove it."

Dorothy pulled back her cloak and revealed the East Marshal star.

He stared at it for a moment before letting out a low whistle. "Well I'll be," he said.

He turned to face the rest of his men, who had followed him into the barn. "Gentlemen, it looks as if fate has smiled upon us yet again. Bring the Marshal to the lab."

Two of the bigger farmers, each a head taller than Dorothy, unlocked her cage and pulled her out.

Now that she was out in the open and no longer contained by steel bars she knew she had prepared her whole life for something like this.

She went limp in their arms and, as they shifted their weight to correct for the sudden increase in hers, she struck out.

She gave the first man a swift kick between the legs and he crumbled instantly to the ground.

She yanked the second man's arm behind his back as she backpedaled quickly and spun him around while he awkwardly tried to regain his footing. As she came back around in a full circle, the first man was already on his hands and knees trying to get up. She delivered a sharp kick to his face sending him back down to the ground.

She had almost thrown the second man off balance when a gunshot reverberated through the barn and a bullet whizzed past her ear.

She let go of the second man and raised her hands.

A sharp blow to the back of her head, probably delivered by the angry second man, forced her down to her hands and knees. She looked up in time to see him winding up to punch her squarely in the face.

"Enough!" yelled Captain Myers. The second man stopped short and stood up straight, sneering down at her.

Captain Meyer shook his head. "She's no good to us if you hit her in the face. We don't have time to wait for the swelling to go down."

He motioned to two more men, who were even bigger than the first two. "Bring her."

She looked up at the two behemoths with a wry smile on her lips. "They sure do grow them big here in OZ. You know what they say about the bigger they are?"

They hesitated for a moment and Captain Myers frowned at them. "She's just a girl."

He looked over at her and his eyes bored straight through her. "And she won't try anything else, will she?"

Dorothy shook her head slightly.

The men came over; each gripped an arm just below her shoulders, and yanked her forcibly to her feet. This time she allowed them to lead her out of the barn without putting up a fight. They followed Captain Myers to a bigger barn adjacent to the one they just left.

Once inside, her mouth fell open at the intricate machinery that filled the entire barn. It hummed and crackled with electricity.

Captain Myers noticed her staring at the scientific and technological marvels on display all around them. "Quite impressive, isn't it?"

Dorothy looked at him. "I thought you were farmers."

Captain Myers smiled. "That's just our cover."

Dorothy looked again around her at all the equipment. "What are you doing?"

"Rather than tell you, how about I show you."

He nodded and the two men dragged her over to a small padded platform about the size of a table. They forced her onto the table and tied her down with leather straps.

She struggled to free herself from the leather straps. But they only grew tighter each time she moved.

Captain Myers stood next to the table and looked down at her.

"You would not believe the years of planning I had to do. All the people I had to pay off, bribe, or threaten so they would help me.

Everything I put together, for the single purpose of kidnapping the East Marshal. And then you literally, land in my own backyard."

She struggled against the leather straps making them even tighter. "What are you going to do to me?"

"I'm not going to do anything to you, Dorothy Gale."

Her eyes grew wide in surprise.

Captain Myers chuckled. "Oh yes, I know exactly who you are. And I must say, you are your father's daughter."

She stopped struggling and stared at him in disbelief. "You know my father?"

He motioned to the equipment around them. "Who do you think built all of this?"

"I want to see my father now!"

His smile faded. "I'm sorry but he was stolen from me."

"Stolen?"

"I'm afraid I don't have time for your questions now. After we're done, I promise to tell you whatever you want to know."

Someone from behind Dorothy clamped a wooden box around her head and latched it shut. With only her head inside the box, her own scream made her ears ring. A rubber hose poked through a hole in the front of the box and brushed against her lips.

Captain Myers voice came to her muffled through the walls of the box. "I suggest you breathe through this for the duration. Please do not move during the procedure. I wouldn't want to have to do this again."

She started to say something in response but then she felt a warm liquid rise up from the back of her head and fill the box. Within seconds, she realized, it would cover her mouth and she would drown in whatever they were pouring into the box. She gripped the rubber tube in her mouth and breathed through it frantically as the warm liquid rose up to cover her face. She closed her eyes just as the liquid enveloped her entire head.

She was unable to gauge how long she had been laying there before someone loosened the leather straps and sat her up. Her head lolled to one side from the weight of the box before someone straightened it and unlatched it.

She felt the box being removed, but something still covered her head that kept her from opening your eyes.

A muted voice sounded like it was being spoken from the distance. "Hold still while we cut this off."

She took a big breath and blinked the way the brightness as they peeled something off her face and removed the breathing tube from her mouth.

She looked around her, slightly disoriented. "What did you do to me?"

Captain Myers held up the plaster casting and inspected it for a moment before looking at her with a smile. "Thank you for not moving while it hardened."

She looked at the plaster casting. It contained the perfect reverse image of her own face. "What are you going to do with that?"

He smiled. "Something amazing."

He motioned to the two big men on either side of her. "Take her to the transfer."

They grabbed her but she dug her heels in the floor and looked at Captain Myers. "You promised to answer my questions."

He smiled. "And I will."

His smile faded. "When we're finished."

The two men wrestled her over to another chair and sat her down again. They took great pleasure in making the straps a little too tight.

Captain Myers placed a leather strap around her head. Copper wires snaked from the strap on her head to a machine that took up half of the wall on one side of the barn. One of the men forced her mouth open while the other shoved a wooden dowel into it like the bit on a horse and strapped it in place around her head. "Only a precaution mind you. Wouldn't want you biting your tongue off. I've found that the body usually spasms when hit with this much voltage."

Tears formed in her eyes. The only thing she could think about was that Nero would somehow save her. He had asked her to put her trust in him. He sounded so sincere and she doubted it the minute he said it, but it was the only hope she could cling to as she waited for this lunatic to electrocute her to death.

Captain Myers walked over to a large switch and placed his hand on the handle. "This might sting a little."

He pulled down on the handle and it felt like every cell in her body was suddenly on fire. The sensation only last for a second because, after that second, she blacked out.

Dorothy coughed in spasms causing dust to lift up from the ground that she was lying face down on. She tried to move, but her body refused to comply. She coughed a couple more times and finally felt the sharp rocks and scratchy straw resolve out of the general tingly sensation that she had felt over her entire body when she first woke up. She wiggled her fingers and, satisfied that she had regained control over her body, placed her hands on the ground and pushed herself up to seated position.

A slight wave of dizziness came over her and she looked down at her body; only to see that while she was unconscious another group of men had seen fit to remove her clothes and dress her in a tight-fitting leather catsuit that left only her neck, head and hands exposed.

This was getting ridiculous. What made everyone in OZ think that, while you were asleep, you needed a complete wardrobe makeover?

She looked around her and saw that she was back in her steel cage. Only this time she was not inside the barn, but outside in a fenced off section of a field. All along the fence, men leaned against it hooting and hollering.

A voice from behind her broke through the loud catcalls of the gathering crowd. "How do you feel?"

She twisted around and saw Captain Myers staring down at her.

"You try to drown me in plaster and then electrocute me. How am I supposed to feel?"

He shrugged his shoulders. "Good enough to fight."

"What are you talking about?"

He pointed over her shoulder. "In the cage across the field is your duplicate. She looks like you, talks like you and even behaves like you. As far as everyone else is concerned, she is you. The only difference between you and her is, she will be under my control."

His smile was not warm. "And when she kills you, she will be the East Marshal. That is unless you think you can defeat somebody that is faster, stronger and, dare I say it, better than you.

Dorothy stood up and glared at him. "I will not play your game."

He motioned behind her with a wave of his hand.

"Your Marshal star is on a little podium in the middle of the field. The first one who gets it and returns to her cage becomes the Marshal."

From somewhere a loud horn sounded and the door to her cage swung open. She looked across the field and saw her intended replacement already running for the podium.

She took off in a flash and forced herself to run as fast as her aching muscles would allow. They were still a bit unresponsive from the electrocution she had endured, but her father's words drifted in from a distant memory, from a time long before she landed in OZ.

Mind over body.

She surged forward and reached the podium half a second after her doppelgänger snatched up the Marshal star and started running back toward her cage.

Dorothy launched herself in the air and tackled the automaton that looked exactly like her.

The star flew into the tall grass as they collapsed to the ground in a heap.

They both sprung to their feet and faced each other.

And froze.

Dorothy studied the automaton. It was like looking in a mirror, only her reflection was backward.

The automaton spun around to kick her, but Dorothy had anticipated this exact move. She was thinking of using it herself.

She countered by grabbing the leg and throwing her opponent off balance and down to the ground. The automaton obviously expected that counter-move and rolled with the momentum back on to her feet.

They both attacked and counter-attacked in a flurry of punches and kicks, neither really landing anything substantial on the other. It was clear they would be unable to surprise each other since they appeared to be the exact same person on the inside.

But how could this be?

She remembered Captain Myers had mentioned her father built all the equipment in the barn. Had he been successful in transferring the human consciousness to an automaton?

Even if he had, why had he done it for the psychotic Captain Myers?

She and her doppelgänger circled each other in the middle of the field, both staring at the other. The automaton moved exactly as she moved. The same mannerisms, the same facial expressions. The couple of times she had come in contact with the automaton's face or hands she noticed the skin was warm and soft. Just like the Alice automaton back at Nero's casino.

They were so much alike she barely had to think when she deflected the attacks from the automaton.

They could do this all day.

Unfortunately, they both couldn't do this all day. She would get tired long before the automaton. She had to do something different. Something she wouldn't think of doing normally. And she had to do it quickly.

While she was trying to think of something, anything, the automaton suddenly changed tactics and ran away from her. In the briefest of moments, she realized it was going for the Marshal star.

She dashed after it and tackled it to the ground by its feet.

They wrestled around in the dirt until Dorothy caught a break and got an arm under the head of the automaton. The voice of Mr. Bart echoed in her head. Subject the joints to strains that they are anatomically and mechanically unable to resist.

She pulled back as hard as she could, the automaton choking and writhing under her killing force.

It was unnerving how human-like the automatons in OZ had become. They could even be killed like humans.

A gunshot echoed over the valley and Dorothy looked up to see Nero holding a revolver in the air. Smoke curled from the tip of the barrel.

"That'll be enough Dorothy."

She released the automaton, which gasped and choked just like a real human. She looked around and saw that Nero's men had rounded up all the farmers and held them together at gunpoint.

Nero holstered his revolver and bent down to pick something up out of the tall grass.

He inspected the star for moment and then looked up at Dorothy. He studied her face and then looked at the automaton and back again to her.

He turned to face Captain Myers. "Which one's which?"

Captain Myers smiled. "You tell me?"

Nero studied them. "Standup. Both of you."

Dorothy stood up slowly, every muscle screaming in agony from the battle she had almost won. She watched as the automaton slowly got to its feet, trying to act as human as possible.

Nero circled them a couple of times, poking and prodding at their faces and inspecting their hands.

"Excellent artisanship, Captain Myers. I am impressed with what you have achieved in so short a time. I can barely tell them apart."

He circled around behind them and looked between them at Captain Myers. "But what about up here?" he said as he poked at the automaton's head. The automaton jerked its head away in reflex just like a human would.

Captain Myers smiled. "Go ahead. Ask them anything."

He circled back around and faced the both of them.

"What is your name?"

The automaton was a split-second quicker in responding as they both answered simultaneously. "Dorothy Gale."

Nero looked seriously from one to the other before locking his eyes on Dorothy. "What was your father's name?"

This time, neither of them let him finish the sentence before they both answered simultaneously, "Benjamin Gale."

Dorothy shot a hard look at the automaton standing next to her. They had managed to copy her memories and personality into the robot. She had to do something else to prove that she was the real Dorothy.

Nero looked over at Captain Myers who was grinning from ear to ear. "This is proving more difficult than I would've expected. You've eliminated the delay for the processing of information."

He looked back at Dorothy as he asked the next question. It was obvious he had already decided who the real Dorothy was.

"What was the last thing I said to you?"

This time, she was a split-second quicker than the automaton. "You told me to trust you."

The other Dorothy responded. "Actually, you winked at me and told me to remember what you said."

He turned to Captain Myers. "Looks like we've got a discrepancy."

Captain Myers was no longer smiling. "It's minor Do you remember the last thing you said to her?"

Nero looked back to the two Dorothys. "Can't say that I do."

"There you go then, Nero. Still a near-perfect copy."

"Let's try a question that's a little less ordinary."

Dorothy swallowed hard and knew that she needed to do something other than answer questions to prove who she was. She glanced down and saw a sharp rock in the dirt in front of her. She bent down, snatched it up in a fluid motion, and held it up for everyone to see. "I can prove who I am right now."

She rolled up the sleeve on her catsuit and scratched the rock across her arm, cutting through skin and drawing blood.

Her adrenaline was running so high; she barely even felt the self-inflicted wound.

She held up her arm for everyone to see but maintained her focus on Captain Myers. "I'd like to see your automaton do that!"

Nero drew his revolver so quickly, she barely even registered his hand had moved when the bullet caught her in the shoulder and spun her down to the ground.

Hot searing pain tore through her body as she gripped her bleeding shoulder.

Nero walked over and looked down at her with a frown. He pointed the revolver at her head and pulled back on the cocking lever.

"I thought I told you to trust me Dorothy."

She barely felt the bullet enter through her eye socket before everything became nothing.

Chapter 4

Dorothy stared down at the hole in the head of the other Dorothy. Copper wires protruded out the gaping gunshot wound Nero had inflicted on the automaton.

What had made him decide the other one wasn't the real Dorothy? That little trick with the rock even had her doubting her own self. Right before Nero shot her, Dorothy was starting to believe that maybe she was the automaton and, because of the memory transfer, only thought she was the real Dorothy.

She looked at Nero who winked at her. "Remember what I said."

"How did you know she was the automaton?"

Nero laughed. "I didn't."

He started to turn away but Dorothy grabbed his arm and pulled him back. "You mean to tell me you decided to shoot first and ask questions later?"

He shrugged his shoulders nonchalantly. "I had a 50-50 chance of getting it right."

"You had a 50-50 chance of getting it wrong!"

He held out the East Marshal star to her. "You still want to see the Wizard?"

Dorothy took the star and searched his face for anything that might tell her she was about to be betrayed again.

"I thought you said you couldn't help me directly."

He hooked a thumb toward the rounded up farmers. "I couldn't let these yokels kill you off before you met with the Wizard now, could I?"

"Why are you helping me?"

"Because Caleb asked me to and any debt he owes is a debt I owe."

She couldn't believe how people in OZ switched from savagery to nobility in the blink of an eye.

Thinking about savagery reminded her how he had treated her the last time. "You told me to trust you but it really looked like you were trying to kill me back in your coliseum."

He smiled a warm smile at her. "Caleb and I had that situation well in hand. Why do you think the control box on your Woodsman was so easy to destroy? Besides, I have the image of a ruthless tyrant to uphold."

"So that whole thing about Caleb disappointing you and sentencing him to die with me was all an act?"

"My mother always wanted me to go into theater. But it would have interfered with my plans to rule the world."

He placed a reassuring hand on her shoulder. "Now let's see about getting you and the Wizard in the same room together."

Nero and Dorothy stood in front of the Flying Monkey Tavern. Nearly all of the paint on the sign had peeled away from years of neglect. The last few bits of faded color were cracked and curled around the edges.

It didn't look like much, but Nero insisted that this was the place they had to go if she wanted to meet the Wizard.

It had taken several hours for Nero and his men to sneak her and her group into Center City unnoticed. During that time, she tried to think about nothing. But there was too much to think about.

A few times Jasper tried to strike up a conversation with her but she waved him away. She was relieved when Nero took her to meet his contact and left the rest of her group with his men in an inn on the outskirts of Center City. It meant she no longer had to respond to questions she did not know the answers to.

Besides, she had plenty of questions of her own.

"Are you sure that someone here can get me in to see the Wizard?"

He looked at Dorothy. "You let me do all the talking in there. And make sure to keep that star hidden. The marshals are not very welcome in Center City."

Dorothy gripped her cloak tighter with one hand.

After everyone seemed to be trying to prevent her from meeting the Wizard, someone was finally helping her.

As he gripped the door handle to the tavern, Nero looked at her one last time. "Remember what I said. Once you get to the Wizard, tell him the Emerald Stallion sends his regards and he will help you."

He yanked on the handle, opened the tavern door and walked down a couple of steps into the darkened bar.

She followed him down the steps and saw that, even in the middle of the day, the tavern was nearly full.

Nero was already in the middle of the room and she hurried to catch up to him when he spun around and pointed at her, yelling loudly enough to make everyone in the room stop talking to each other. "Grab her! She's the East Marshal!"

Several hands instantly clamped onto Dorothy. Nero walked up and ripped open her cloak allowing everyone to see the shiny East Marshal star pinned to her chest. Despite Nero's announcement, several people gasped when they saw the star.

He turned in a slow circle as he addressed the crowd. "I overheard her talking about assassinating the Wizard. At this very moment my men are closing in on the rest of her little rebellious strike force."

He completed his circle and faced her. "Thanks to the vigilance of the people of Center City, your plan to overthrow the great and powerful Wizard of OZ and force our peaceful city into war with the outer territories has failed."

The deep rumble of a voice came from right behind her. "What do we do with her?"

From all around the tavern voices shouted, "kill her," and "string her up," and the more unnerving, "burn her."

Nero looked at her with a hard stare. "I have a better idea. Let's turn her over to the Wizard and collect a reward."

This resulted in shouts of jubilation from the half-inebriated crowd.

Nero smiled as he looked around at the crowd he had worked up so easily, but when he looked back at Dorothy, his face switched instantly to one of alarm.

He raised a hand up and shouted, "No!"

In that same moment, Dorothy felt a sharp pain in the back of her head followed by a flash of white light that washed out the scene before her.

She felt her face hit the floor and tried to focus on a boot heel right in front of her.

Her eyes refused to cooperate and the mud-caked boot blurred before it faded into darkness.

Chapter 5

Water forced itself into Dorothy's nose and mouth, waking her up and choking her. When her coughing fit ended, she felt a hand grab her hair and lift her head up. Fingers pulled on her eyelids as a man stared closely at her face.

"Again," the man said.

He let go of her hair and her head drooped back down, her chin touching her chest. She leaned forward slightly and strained against the ropes that bound her to the chair.

Another bucket full of water was thrown onto her. Only this time she was awake and anticipated it quickly enough to hold her breath.

The man grabbed her hair again and lifted her head. She glared at him and he smiled.

He turned away from her and said, "She's ready."

He stood up and stepped to the side.

Behind him was another man who silently watched her for a moment before he squatted down in front of her.

"Who are you working for?"

She coughed up a little more water before speaking. "I'm here to see the Wizard."

The man stood up to his full height. "You found him, but I'm afraid your little assassination plot didn't go as planned."

"I'm not here to assassinate you, I have a message."

"And what kind of message would someone like me want from someone like you?"

"The Emerald Stallion sends his regards."

The Wizard smiled. "The Emerald Stallion, eh? Now that's a horse of a different color. He doesn't hand out his secret pass code to just anyone. I take it he arranged this meeting?"

She nodded her head.

He looked at his assistant. "Well? Untie her already."

The relief on her shoulders was immediate. She rubbed her wrists, trying to bring circulation back to her hands as she regarded the Wizard. He looked to be in his late twenties, if not his early thirties. Everyone told her that OZ had been built specifically for him. But this place was older than she was. This meant he would have been no more than a 10-year-old boy when they built OZ.

"You're much younger than I expected."

The Wizard smiled. "From all the stories I've heard of your exploits, so are you."

Dorothy's brow furrowed "My exploits?"

He began to pace about as he talked, alternating from looking at her to looking around the room.

"You killed the East Marshal. Congratulations by the way. You formed an alliance with Chambers. Not an easy task mind you, they are a very private group. You escaped from Nero's coliseum. I assume you had inside help to accomplish that feat."

She nodded; surprised to hear all of her accidental accomplishments portrayed as though they were carefully planned.

"I thought so. You also stole the West Marshal's fastest airship. And you did this all in a matter of days."

She smiled sheepishly. "I can explain all of that."

He waved his hand dismissively. "No need to explain anything. You are the East Marshal. You can do whatever you want."

Her shoulders drooped. "If only that were true."

"Ah, yes. You can do everything except for why you've come to see me."

She fixed her steely gaze on the Wizard. "I want… I need to get out of OZ."

He waggled his finger. "Haven't you heard? OZ is inescapable."

"Have I asked for something the great and powerful Wizard can't do?"

"I can do many, many things. Getting out of OZ is not one of them."

Dorothy's heart sank. "So, you can't help me."

"I did not say that. But I would wager that is not what you really want."

"It's what I want."

"And why do you want this so much?"

"I have to get back to New Kansas."

"And what's in New Kansas that is so terribly important?"

"Well, nothing really. But it will be the first place my father will try to contact me again."

He pointed a finger at the ceiling. "Ahh, now we've gotten to what you really want."

"Of course I want to find my father. But I have to get out of OZ to do that."

"So I take it he is not in OZ?"

"He is in OZ. But this place is too big to search for him on my own. And I lost the only thing that can guide me to him."

The Wizard shook his head. "No you haven't."

"You found my necklace?"

"No, but I can find your father."

Dorothy's heart skipped a beat. "How?"

"It is not hard for someone as, shall we say, connected as I am. But first you must tell me that this is what you really want."

She swallowed, forcing her heart back down her throat and into her chest. "Yes. Yes. That is what I really want."

He smiled. "Excellent. Let's talk about my fee."

Chapter 6

The guard stationed in front of the guest quarters unlocked and opened the door while the other two guards ushered Dorothy in through the threshold.

Once inside, the guards let her go and quickly exited, locking the door behind them.

She placed a hand on the wall to steady herself, but she was a second too late. Her legs gave out and she started to crumple to the floor when someone reached out and held her up.

She refocused her eyes and saw the golden furry face of Caleb.

He looked at her with concern. "Are you okay?"

She wanted to say she was fine.

But she wasn't.

What the Wizard had asked from her in return for his help was something she could never do.

Her knees buckled again and Caleb gripped her arms tightly, supporting her. "Jasper, help me get her over to the chair."

Together they guided her over and sat her down gently in the chair.

All the emotions she had kept bottled up for years bubbled to the surface and spilled over. And she began to cry.

Caleb knelt down beside her. "What did he ask from you?"

She looked at him through the tears. "I've come all this way."

Jasper hopped about excitedly. "What does he want you to do?"

She wrapped her arms around Caleb and buried her face into his shoulder. "I can't do it. I can't do what he wants me to do. I can't... I can't save my father."

She cried harder knowing that she had failed to find her father and, now that she was trapped in OZ, would never get the chance to see him ever again.

He hugged her tightly and stroked the back of her head. "It's okay. We will find another way. We don't need the Wizard's help to find your father."

Caleb's shoulder was getting damp from her tears. She leaned back, sniffed deeply, and wiped her nose. "This place is just too big. We can spend the rest of our lives looking and never..." Her words faded to silence.

Caleb smiled and pushed aside an errant strand of hair that had fallen in front of her face. "Nero's resources are almost as vast as the Wizard's. He can help us. In fact, I wouldn't be surprised if the Wizard asked for Nero's help after you paid his price."

Jasper hovered around them and bounced nervously on the tips of his toes. "What was his price?"

She looked at Jasper and felt her soul darken as she repeated the Wizard's request. "He wants me to kill the West Marshal."

Jasper clapped his hands and spun around in place. "I knew it!"

Caleb shot him a disapproving look. "Not right now Jasper."

Jasper bounced in close. "He always does this."

Dorothy wiped away another tear. "He always asks someone to kill?"

Jasper's face could barely contain his grin. "No. He always sets his price too high and never has to follow through with his deal."

Caleb frowned. "Then what are you so excited about?"

Jasper stopped hopping about and his face grew serious. "Because we got him this time. After we kill the West Marshal, he will have to get us out of OZ or nobody will come to him for a favor again. His magical hold over the people of OZ will be lost."

Caleb shook his head. "Haven't you been listening? We're not killing anyone."

"But we have to. After we're done with the West Marshal, we'll either be out of OZ or the great and powerful Wizard will be knocked down from his pedestal. It's a win-win either way."

Caleb stood up to allow his height to intimidate Jasper. "We've already told you, we're not killing the West Marshal."

Jasper looked from Caleb to Dorothy and then back to Caleb. "But we have to."

Dorothy tuned them out as they continued to argue back and forth about whether they would go and kill the West Marshal or not. She didn't have the heart to tell them that the Wizard had renegotiated her side of the agreement, since getting out of OZ was impossible.

The back of her mind tickled at a memory. Some tiny little fact tossed out in the middle of some forgotten conversation clawed its way to the surface. It screamed for attention as she tried to focus on what her subconscious seemed to already know.

Her head snapped to attention as a memory came into a sharp focus.

She cut off the argument between the two boys and stared at Caleb. "Back at the coliseum Nero said that he raised you from an infant."

Caleb nodded his head. "He rescued me when some bandits killed everyone in my town."

Dorothy stared deep into his eyes looking for any sign of deceit. "Do you know a way out of OZ?"

Caleb averted his gaze and shook his head. "No."

"But I met you a few years ago back in New Kansas."

"Right. You saved my life from those hooligans in that back alley."

"New Kansas is not inside OZ."

Caleb's face changed. He had been caught in a lie and he knew it.

Jasper's face registered utter confusion as he stared at Caleb. "You've been outside of OZ?"

Caleb raised his hands in front of him. "Nero found a way out…"

Jasper balled his hands into fists as he shouted at Caleb. "You mean to tell me we've gone through all of this and you could've just walked us out?"

Caleb responded to Jasper's outrage without taking his eyes off Dorothy. "We used it a few times. But the security breach was discovered and sealed. We never found another way out. You have to believe me."

Jasper launched himself at Caleb and tackled him to the ground. Caleb flung him off easily and regained his feet. Jasper scrambled back to his own feet and crouched low, ready to charge at Caleb again.

Caleb emitted a low growl and bared his teeth.

Dorothy stepped in between them. "We are also not going to kill each other."

She turned to face Jasper. "Caleb is helping us, he is not the enemy."

Jasper pointed an accusing finger at Caleb. "He lied to us."

Dorothy shook her head. "He said the security hole they found was plugged up."

"Maybe he's still lying."

"Everything he's done has been to help us. What could he possibly gain by lying to us?"

Jasper stepped forward and back nervously. "He's just waiting for the cool down period to run out so he can kill you and claim the East Marshal star for himself."

Caleb responded with another low guttural growl.

Dorothy held her hands out to stop them from charging at each other again. "That's enough! Both of you."

Someone half coughed behind her and she turned on them. "What do you want!?"

The guard, despite being nearly twice her size, took a step backward. "There is someone asking to see you."

She shook her head, not understanding. "Asking for me? Who?"

A tiny head poked around the edge of the open door.

She recognized his face immediately and, while it could have been any number of people with the same face, she knew instantly who it was.

"Munch!"

He stepped fully into view, but did not smile. He waited until the guard left and heard the door lock engaged.

Dorothy rushed over and gave him a big hug; which he did not return. She sensed his unease and sat back on her heels to look at him. "What's the matter Munch?"

He looked down at his feet and took something out of his pocket. "I have something for you."

He lifted his hand and opened it.

Her emerald necklace!

She lifted the heart-shaped necklace by the chain and let it spin in front of her face. "Where did you find it?"

He continued to stare at his feet. "One of my brothers took it from you without us knowing."

He looked up at her, tears welling up in his eyes. "I am truly sorry."

She smiled. "It's okay Munch. You brought it back to me."

He wiped at the corners of his eyes. "My brother has been punished for his actions."

She barely heard what he said as she looked at the connection with her father that had been restored. It no longer mattered how big OZ was, she could find her father.

She glanced around the room and saw a mirror hanging on the wall.

She pointed to the mirror while looking at Jasper. "Get that mirror and put it on the floor."

"Why?"

"Just do it Jasper."

"Okay, okay. Whatever."

While Jasper placed the mirror on the floor, Dorothy popped the emerald heart out of the necklace.

Caleb knelt down beside her at the mirror. "What are you doing?"

She looked up at him, her heart pounding a fast rhythm. "Looking for my father."

She placed the emerald on the center of the mirror and spun it.

Everyone watched with rapt attention as the emerald slowed and stopped.

Jasper whispered, "What is it supposed to be doing?"

Dorothy looked in the direction the tip of the heart pointed. "It's pointing directly at my father."

Caleb stood up and walked over to look out the window.

He turned back to Dorothy. "You know what else it's pointing at?"

Dorothy stood up and walked over to join Caleb at the window.

"What is…" The rest of the words stuck in her throat and her heart sank as the realization of what she was looking at dawned on her.

Even from this distance, it looked menacing and foreboding.

It seemed to taunt her from the edge of the horizon. As if daring her to come and rescue her father. Laughing in her face because it knew she never stood a chance at succeeding.

For a brief moment, when Munch handed her the necklace, she thought finding her father would be easy.

It appeared that nothing in OZ was ever easy.

She glanced back at the heart lying in the middle of the mirror and traced the imaginary line it made, hoping she'd misjudged the direction it faced the first time.

There was no denying it.

The emerald heart pointed directly at the West Marshal's compound.

Chapter 7

Jasper paced back and forth.

It had been over an hour since Dorothy went to the Wizard to tell him she would fulfill her end of the bargain as long as he guaranteed to fulfill his. The automatons remained outside the castle, locked in a barn and shut down, and Munch was sent home.

Jasper and Caleb were the only two left to wait for her.

Caleb was nestled in the windowsill and stared out at the West Marshal's compound in the distance. Neither had spoken to the other after Dorothy left the room.

Caleb stopped him on his hundredth circuit around the room. "Can you please stop pacing about?"

"Why isn't she back yet?"

Caleb shrugged his shoulders. "I'm not sure."

"Well, I can't stay here."

Caleb looked at him with an amused expression on his face. "And where would you go?"

"Anywhere is better than here."

Caleb motioned with an open hand toward the door. "The guards aren't going to just let you wander around the castle."

Jasper smiled. "They can't stop me."

"Even if that were true, what happens when you get caught or they notice you're missing?"

"I'll be back before they even know I'm gone. I just need to feel like I have some freedom."

Jasper ran over and banged on the door. "Guard!"

He stepped back as the door opened up and the bigger of the two guards leaned in. "What do you want?"

Jasper crossed his legs. "I need a chamber pot."

The guard rolled his eyes. "I hate dealing with commoners. Come with me, we have a flushing toilet."

Jasper smiled at the guard. "Perfect."

Jasper followed the guard as they walked down the hallway and around the corner. The guard stopped by a small door and pointed. "It's in there."

He smiled at the guard. "I won't be long."

The guard frowned. "You better not be."

Jasper closed the door behind him, but could not find any way to lock it.

It didn't matter. He didn't need very much time for what he had planned. He glanced at the ceiling and smiled when he saw the ventilation shaft. If he stood on the edge of the toilet, he could just reach the lip of the open shaft.

In a matter of seconds, he lifted himself completely into the shaft and worked his way on his belly toward the light at the other end of the tunnel.

There were several wrought iron grates spaced evenly along one side of the tunnel. As he passed each grate, he peaked into the room it opened to.

At the third grate, he saw Caleb still sitting in the windowsill. He suppressed the urge to call down to Caleb and gloat that he was wandering around the castle on his own.

As he continued to crawl, he heard voices murmuring up through a vent ahead of him. He shuffled closer and peeked in.

Nero was talking to one of the natives of OZ. The dark-skinned man, adorned with feathers and bones, sat cross-legged on the floor. Rather than looking at Nero while he spoke to him, the native had his eyes closed and rocked back and forth.

Nero watched the native rocking back and forth as he spoke. "She is on her way."

The native did not even acknowledge Nero was in the room as he replied. "You really think she is the key to conquering OZ?"

"Of that, there is no question. As soon as you kill her and take the star, you will proclaim yourself ruler of OZ. The North will fall instantly under the threat of invasion; your army will be unstoppable."

"And how am I supposed to deal with her?"

"I have sent a package filled with the venom from a unique and very deadly spider found only here in OZ."

"I know of it."

"It will be clean and quick. But not painless."

Jasper clamped a hand over his own mouth to keep himself from yelling out in surprise.

He had to tell Caleb what he just overheard and warn Dorothy.

He shuffled backward in the shaft until he got to the grate overlooking their room. He pushed with his feet and the grate popped out, clattering loudly to the floor.

Caleb leaped from the windowsill and stared up at him. Jasper dropped down to the floor and looked around the room.

"She's not back yet?"

Caleb shook his head. "Not yet."

"We have to warn her."

"Warn her of what?"

"I just overheard him talking. She's walking into a trap."

Caleb gripped him by the shoulders and shook him slightly to refocus his attention. "You're not making any sense. Who did you hear talking?"

He looked into Caleb's cat-like eyes. "Nero."

Caleb's eyebrows lifted in surprise. "Nero's here? What did he say exactly?"

"She can't go. It's a trap."

"What did he say?"

"Nero sent some kind of spider poison to the West Marshal. She's going to kill the East Marshal and start a war against the Northern Territories. We have to warn her. She's in danger."

Caleb gripped his shoulders tighter, his claws digging slightly into his skin. "You're right. She is in danger."

Dorothy let the guards lead her back to the room were Caleb and Jasper waited.

She hadn't felt good about lying to the Wizard, but agreeing to his fee was the only way that any of them would leave the castle alive.

She had no intention of killing the West Marshal and bringing back the star for him. She had her emerald heart and could use that to find her father. She didn't need the Wizard's help any longer.

When she got to the West Marshal's compound, she would find her father and together they would escape from OZ.

In addition, she would bring Caleb and Jasper with her out of OZ. After everything they had done for her, she could not leave them here.

That was not something you did to friends.

The door opened and she walked into the room to find Caleb still seated on the windowsill.

He glanced over at her and smiled. He waited for the guards to leave and close the door before he spoke. "Do you think he believed you?"

"He's providing us an armed escort all the way to the western border. What do you think?"

She looked around the room, but Caleb was the only one there. "Where's Jasper?"

Caleb shrugged his shoulders. "He left a little while ago to go to the toilet and never came back."

"How long ago was that?"

"Almost half an hour. He did mention something about sneaking out of the castle. Maybe he escaped and took off."

"He wouldn't have just left."

"I wouldn't think too much of it."

Dorothy shook her head. "He wouldn't have done that without saying goodbye. We had become friends."

Caleb walked up and held her hands in his. "It's often hard to tell who your friends are here in OZ."

He leaned forward and gazed deeply into her eyes. "Your friends are the ones who don't abandon you when you need them the most."

Chapter 8

Dorothy crossed her arms across her chest and tried very hard to understand what the Commander was telling her. "I was promised an armed escort."

The Commander gave her a sheepish grin. "I'm sorry. This is as far any of my men are willing to go without native support."

She glanced sideways at the "native support". The two dark-skinned men, decorated with feathers and the bones and teeth of dead animals, sat facing each other. Their eyes were open, but they did not see each other. The only sound coming from them was a low rhythmic hum that matched their slight rocking motion.

She looked back at the Commander. "What are they doing?"

"They are trying to contact other natives in the Western Territories. They are checking to see if there is any safe passage for us."

She looked back at the two chanting men. "They can do that?"

The Commander regarded the two men. "They have no written language and no records showing what they know. But I have seen them do amazing things that can only be classified as witchcraft."

"They don't seem like an evil people."

"They're not. Unfortunately, witchcraft is the only word we have for what they seem to be able to do."

The two men suddenly went silent. One of them looked up at the Commander and addressed him in perfect English. "We will go no further."

The Commander looked back at Dorothy. "That means we turn back here. If you want to keep going, you can do so alone."

She could barely contain her anger. "You would go against a direct order from the Wizard because of what they said?"

The Commander looked at her without the hint of any emotion on his stolid face. "Even the Wizard would not go against native advice."

Caleb wandered over and stood next to her as they watched the soldiers gather up their belongings and turn around the carriage to begin the long march back to Center City.

The younger of the two natives walked up to her. "Please wait a short while after you've lost sight of the soldiers before continuing on your journey. There is someone who will be joining you."

She looked at the native; her eyebrows furrowed in confusion. "Who is joining us?"

He smiled. "A friend."

"How do you know?"

"He spoke to us."

She exchanged a quick glance with Caleb.

"Did you just speak with him telepathically?"

The native smiled wider. "No. He told us back in the castle."

Dorothy and Caleb looked at each other as the native jogged to catch up with the departing soldiers.

They stood by the side of the road and watched them march back toward Center City, leaving her and Caleb all alone in a treacherous land. Earlier, she overheard a couple of the soldiers discuss the possibility they might have to cross over into the Western Territories. One of them remarked that he would rather be dropped in the Eastern Territories naked and wounded than venture into the Western Territories fully armed and with highly trained soldiers.

It did not sound like a place she should go by herself, or even with one other person.

Dorothy shook her head. "Do you think they knew they would be turning back before we got to the border?"

Caleb nodded his head. "I'm sure they knew before they even offered to take us."

"Then why wouldn't they let us bring the Woodsman and Scarecrow?"

"There are barely any automatons in the Western Territories. We would stick out like a sore thumb."

After the soldiers disappeared over the crest of a hill, she looked at Caleb. "What do we do now?"

Caleb sat down and leaned against a tree. "We wait."

"How long should we wait?"

He looked up at her. "Our cryptic friend implied it wouldn't take too long."

"Who do you think it is? Do you think it might be Jasper?"

He looked down the road the soldiers had taken. "I don't think so."

"Why not?"

He pointed in the direction he was looking. "For one thing, he's too short."

She followed the direction of his finger. The lone traveler noticed her and waved.

She ran down the dusty road to meet him. "Munch! What are you doing here?"

He smiled up at her. "I knew the natives would turn back before the border and the soldiers would follow them. Your predecessor took me with her a few times while visiting her sister, so I know my way around the Western Territories. I thought you might want a guide."

Caleb eyed Munch suspiciously. "You can get us into the Western Territories?"

Munch practically had to look straight up to meet Caleb's gaze and did his best to hide the fear in his eyes. "In a manner of speaking."

Dorothy placed a hand on Caleb's chest. "Munch is a friend. You said so yourself, friends do not abandon friends when they need them most. And we need to get over that border."

Munch dropped his pack on the ground and started digging through it. He pulled out two loaves of bread and a round of cheese.

"Eat now. You will not have any chance to eat during the trip."

When Munch said he knew how to get them over the border by using the phrase "in a manner of speaking" he was not kidding.

They had just finished eating when a horse-drawn cart overloaded with manure pulled to a stop in front of them.

Munch spoke to the driver briefly, handing him two small pouches. He walked back to Dorothy and Caleb.

"I have paid the driver and he will pay the border guard."

Caleb pointed at the manure-filled cart. "I am not riding in that."

Munch looked up at him. "Getting into the land in the west is hard. One of the few things that actually crosses over the border on a regular basis is fertilizer. Not only will it get us in but he will take us all the way to the fields just outside the West Marshal's compound. We should get there just before nightfall and we won't have to wait long before crossing the lake to the castle."

Caleb shook his head. "There's no way I'm crawling around in any of that."

Dorothy placed a hand on his shoulder. "Is it the only way we can get across the border and travel safely through the West?"

Munch nodded. "Yes. There is a standing order to kill the East Marshal on sight. We have to keep her hidden."

She smiled. "It won't be that bad. After a couple of washings you will be as good as new."

Caleb looked at her. "You don't have to wash yourself with your tongue."

She was about to respond with a witty retort when Munch interrupted their pending argument as he yanked three large burlap sacks from his pack.

"Nobody is going to have to wash anything. We will be inside of these."

The driver called over to them from the manure cart. "I have a schedule. If you're not coming, I don't offer refunds."

Caleb stared long and hard at her until finally she grinned and raised her hands in a "what can you do?" gesture.

Twenty minutes later, all three of them were enclosed in burlap sacks and buried deep in the manure.

The cart started back up on its journey to the border and beyond. It jostled and wobbled for a few moments before it finally settled into the ruts on the road.

After the first fifteen minutes, Dorothy hardly noticed the smell. After nearly two hours, she had become quite comfortable and dozed off to sleep.

Every now and then, when the wheel closest to her hit a rock, it would jolt her awake. But the womb-like embrace of the manure, and the gentle rocking of the carriage, would lull her back to sleep.

She was asleep when the cart jerked to a stop.

The sudden lack of movement woke her up.

The sound of voices getting closer brought her fully awake.

She could just make out the muffled voices of the driver and someone who sounded like a border guard.

"We thank you for your generous contribution to the border guard's Christmas ball. But I have a job to do."

The cart rocked as someone stepped up on to the back and scrambled over the pile of manure. She lay perfectly still and felt the pressure of the manure on her legs increase as someone walked over her. The driver's voice raised an octave as he tried to coax the border guard down. "As you can see, all I have is a shipment of fertilizer for the Marshal's fields."

"Then it wouldn't bother you if I did this." Dorothy nearly cried out when the blade of a saber pierced the only thing between her and the manure, and sliced through the air, half an inch in front of her nose. The blade retreated and bits of manure dropped through the new hole in the sack. The pressure on her legs shifted and the cart rocked again as the guard jumped down to the ground. "This one is clear. Open the gate."

Within moments, the cart lurched forward and they passed over the border into the Western Territories.

Chapter 9

A loud ripping sound startled Dorothy.

The cart had stopped sometime before and the only thing she heard was muffled voices and the slight rocking of the cart as people moved around on the pile of manure above her.

Dorothy blinked her eyes open just as the burlap sack split apart to let the afternoon sun wash over her. She raised a hand to shield her eyes.

Munch appeared in her line of sight and held out a small stack of clothes to her. "Put these on."

She blinked a few more times to get her eyes used to the blinding sunlight.

She took the clothes and inspected them. They were some kind of uniform. Munch held up a second stack of clothing tied together with string. "As soon as the uniform is on, wear this over it."

She took the second bundle of clothing and looked at Munch. "What are these?"

"As soon as we are inside the compound we will need to look like we belong there."

She looked up and saw that Munch was already wearing his uniform and behind him, Caleb held a jumpsuit up against himself. They looked to be a couple of sizes too small.

She untied the string on the second bundle and unfolded it to reveal a jumpsuit just like the one Caleb was putting on. Embroidered on the back where the words "Agricultural Volunteer".

She held it up to inspect it. "What about this?"

"As long as we are outside the compound, we need to look like we belong here."

She glanced around and saw they were on the edge of a massive field. Workers, all wearing the same jumpsuits Munch handed her, were bent over harvesting crops by hand.

"Are all of these people volunteers?"

Munch looked around him and then back at her. "It sure beats volunteering in the mines," he said.

Caleb had finished wriggling into his jumpsuit and walked up to them. He inspected the bits of fur that poked out through the stretched seams. "It's a bit tight."

Munch frowned. "I didn't really know your size."

Caleb looked over at Dorothy just as she finished donning her own jumpsuit over the uniform. "Hers fits perfectly."

Munch shrugged his shoulders. "I'm the East Marshal's personal tailor."

Dorothy realized that she and Munch had uniforms, but he only handed Caleb a jumpsuit. "What about a uniform for Caleb?"

Munch grimaced. "There's no way he could pull off looking like a guard. Not with that face. He will have to be our prisoner as we make our way through the compound."

As she looked around her at the workers in the fields, she noticed something was missing. "Where are all the guards?"

"Everyone works here based on the 'on your' system."

"Don't you mean the honor system?"

"Nope. It is definitely an 'on your' system. If you do not pull your own weight out here in the fields then you are 'on your' way to the mines. The mines are where you'll find the guards."

"Why do they choose to live here?"

Munch laughed. "Nobody chooses to live here. The border is heavily guarded with most of the guns pointing in. Besides, there are not many places in OZ for someone to go to for a better life."

She untied the other bundle and began dressing in the uniform.

Caleb tugged at his jumpsuit and shifted around uncomfortably. "How long do I need to wear this thing?"

"Just until nightfall. I got us a farming detail on the north side of the compound. After everyone retires to the campsite at sundown, we will sneak out and make our way…"

A large man in a different colored jumpsuit called over to them from a nearby horse-drawn carriage, interrupting Munch. "Hey you! With the fur cap!"

They all turned to look at him. The man's eyes locked onto Caleb and his face registered surprise. "Whoa! Hey. Thought you were wearing a hat. Sorry."

Munch stepped forward. "What do you want?"

The man jumped down from the carriage and strode over.

"We have stump removal in the southern fields. I saw this guy's jumpsuit busting at the seams and knew we could use the muscle."

Munch shook his head. "He's already on a scheduled detail. You'll have to look for your muscle somewhere else."

The large man stepped closer and pointed to his own chest. "You see the color of my jumpsuit? That means I am a volunteer director. Furry face here comes with me."

"We came here together…"

The director parroted Munch with a high-pitched whiny voice. "We came here together."

He stabbed a finger at Munch's chest. "Listen here shrimp, unless you want to work the mines I suggest you and your girlfriend run along."

Caleb emitted a low growl.

Munch looked at him. "He's right, Caleb. I was out of line. You go with the director here and we will catch up with you later. You can meet us at the North Camp at sundown."

The director smiled; satisfied he had won the fight. He looked at Caleb, sticking out his bottom lip in an exaggerated pout. "I'm afraid fuzzball here will have to stay in South Camp until morning."

He stopped mocking Caleb and his face became serious. "When curfew is lifted at sunup, you can meet back up with your friends."

The director jumped back up on top of the carriage and grabbed the reins. "Let's go. We're burning precious daylight."

Caleb looked back at Dorothy as he climbed up into the waiting carriage. Before the door on the carriage was closed, the director yelled at the horses and they departed for the opposite end of the compound.

Munch took her arm and led her to another waiting carriage. "Come on, Dorothy."

"What if…"

He gripped her arm tighter. "It is not safe to talk now. Just work the fields until sundown and I will come find you in the camp."

Dorothy sat down between two other volunteers. When the door closed and the carriage jerked to a start, she realized that Munch had not gotten on with her.

A half hour later, the carriage stopped.

Volunteers scrambled out, sweeping Dorothy with them, as volunteer directors stepped out of the fields to greet them and bark imperceptible orders.

One of the more aggressive volunteer directors shoved Dorothy toward the field. She lost her footing and went down on all fours.

The volunteer director twisted fistfuls of her jumpsuit in his hands and lifted her to her feet. "You can rest at sundown."

He shoved a sling bag into her hands and pointed to the ripening tomatoes in the field in front of her. "They're not going to harvest themselves."

Dorothy spent the afternoon hunched over, selecting ripened tomatoes, and shoving them in her bag. Any time she tried to stand up and stretch her aching back muscles a volunteer director hurled insults at her.

She was relieved when the sun dipped below the horizon and volunteers rushed past her to claim the precious few seats in the carriages back to the North Camp. By the time Dorothy made it to the pickup area, people were hanging out the windows and clinging to the sides of the three carriages.

The driver of the first carriage called down to her. "Hurry up and find a perch. We're leaving."

She shook her head. "I'll wait for the next trip."

The driver laughed along with a few of the volunteers in his carriage. "There ain't no next trip. Get on."

A volunteer hanging off the side of the carriage shuffled half an inch to her left and looked down at Dorothy. "You can fit right here."

She hopped up and grabbed the railing with one hand since there was not enough room to grab it with both. "Thank you."

The volunteer who had made room for her smiled. "We have to stick together."

The driver whipped the horses and hollered, "Giddy up!"

It took every ounce of strength in her exhausted muscles not to fall off as the carriage lurched into motion.

By the time they made it to the camp, she had to force her fingers to let go of the railing. As soon as she dropped to the ground she wobbled unsteadily and her legs started to buckle.

The other volunteer grabbed her elbow and steadied her. "Are you new to the fields?"

Dorothy looked at her and nodded.

The woman smiled. "If you think you're sore now, wait 'til tomorrow when you have to do this all over again."

Not if Munch finds me tonight, she thought to herself, but dared not speak it aloud.

The woman pointed to a line of volunteers that seemed to be getting longer with each passing second. "That line will get you some soup. I would not comment on what it looks like to the chef. That only seems to upset him." Then she pointed in different directions around the camp. "Over there are the toilets. That way is the sleeping tents. Boys on the right; girls on the left. Breakfast is served half hour before sun up. Don't miss it; it really is the most important meal of the day."

And with that, the woman let go of Dorothy and ran to get her place in the soup line. In the time it took Dorothy to blink, twenty more people got in line behind her.

By the time she made it to the soup line, she lost count of how many people were between her and the young woman who helped her.

Despite the large number of volunteers, the line moved quickly. It did not take long to grab a plate with slop on it and move on to find somewhere to eat.

There was no designated dining area. No long tables with benches, like those in Chambers. Everybody was expected to grab his or her plate and find some unoccupied patch of dirt, an activity that proved far more difficult than she would have expected. Each time she approached a group, they eyed her suspiciously, forcing her to move along and find somewhere else to eat.

She was just about ready to give up and toss her cold slop into a garbage bin when a familiar voice called out to her. "Dorothy."

She turned as Munch ran up to her.

She smiled; glad to have a friend for supper.

As soon as he caught up to her, he grabbed her plate, tossed it in the bushes and pulled her after him as he continued to walk quickly. "We have to get out of here before curfew is enforced."

Dorothy dug in her heels trying to slow him down. "We can't leave without Caleb."

Munch pulled harder to keep them walking at a fast pace. "He's stuck at the other camp. There is no way he can get to us. Nevertheless, we cannot stay here. When they do morning roll call, they will discover we don't belong here. We will never get another chance to leave."

"Is Caleb going to be okay?"

"If he is smart, and I think he is, he will get out of there before morning roll call. For now, all we can do is what we came here to do."

They kept low as they ran through the bushes.

When they reached the edge of camp, Munch knelt on one knee and peered through the branches. He cursed silently under his breath and pointed to someone standing twenty yards away.

"The guard's out early."

He dug around in his pack and retrieved a long strap of leather that had been fashioned into a sling.

He selected a medium-sized rock from the ground and tucked it into the sling's pouch.

He crooked his finger through the loop at one end and gripped the other end with his thumb. He waited until the guard turned away from them before he stood up, swinging the sling several times over his head. At the precise moment, he let go of the thumb strap so that the rock sailed directly at its target. The guard went down hard.

She couldn't believe her eyes.

"Munch, all that talk back at your house about lacking courage and never venturing out of your walled city, yet you know all these people, you got us over the border, you made us uniforms and now you are taking out guards with a sling. Where did you learn to do all this?"

Munch gave her a knowing smile. "Things are not always what they seem in OZ."

He grabbed her hand and pulled her with him as he ran out of the camp.

They kept running until she was gulping for air, her muscles screaming for oxygen.

"We have to stop. Munch, please, I need to rest."

He looked around them and slowed down. "I think we've gone far enough. You can rest for a couple of minutes, but we are almost there."

Dorothy collapsed to the ground and sucked in as much air as she could in the shortest time possible. She breathed so heavily and so quickly, she thought she was going to hyperventilate.

She forced herself to take slower and deeper breaths as the thumping of her heart lessened in her chest.

Munch unfolded a piece of paper and studied it in the dim moonlight. During the time they had been running, he had looked at this paper several times.

"What is that?"

Munch didn't look at her but continued to alternate between studying the map and looking around him.

"It's a map showing me where the land bridge is."

"What land bridge?"

He continued to study the map and look around. "The West Marshal's compound is surrounded by a lake that is a mile wide in every direction. Part of the lake has a land bridge we can use to walk across."

"I know how to swim."

Munch stopped looking at his map and made direct eye contact with her. "Do you want to swim through snake infested waters?"

She shook her head.

He returned his attention back to the map. "That's what I thought."

He looked up and squinted into the darkness. He referred back to his map and then broke into a large smile.

He folded the map up and tucked it back into the pocket of his jumpsuit.

"We are almost there. Are you ready to keep going?"

She stood up. "Lead the way."

Ten minutes later Dorothy and Munch stood on the shore of a massive lake.

There had been no exaggeration on Munch's part as it certainly looked to extend a mile in every direction around the compound that was dimly lit from within by torches and gaslights.

Everything was exactly as Munch had described it.

Except for one thing.

Even in the faint glow of the moon they could tell, there was no land bridge.

Chapter 10

Munch paced up and down the shore, alternating his gaze between the map and their surroundings.

"According to the map, the land bridge is right here."

Dorothy placed a hand on his shoulder. "Maybe the map is wrong."

He jerked his shoulder away from her hand and waved the map in her face. "I paid too much for it to be wrong!"

"Maybe the land bridge doesn't exist."

He crumpled the map up and threw it out into the water. "Ya think?"

The map bobbed around among the waves for a little bit before the parchment soaked up enough water to sink out of sight.

She looked out across the water. "There has to be another way to get across."

"There isn't."

"We can swim across. Maybe the snakes won't bother us."

He shook his head. "It won't work."

"Sure it will. All we have to do is…"

He turned on her and screamed in frustration, "I can't swim!"

He tore off his backpack and threw it out into the lake. It hit the water with a faint splash, but did not sink right away. He laughed sarcastically. "Even my backpack knows how to swim."

He sat down abruptly and placed his head in his hands. "I am so sorry Dorothy. I have failed."

She sat down beside him, placed an arm reassuringly around his shoulders and pulled him close. "No you haven't. Look at where we are. You got us to the West Marshal's compound."

She pointed across the water at the massive multistory castle. "That is the finish line."

He looked out over the water; a tear glistened on his cheek in the moonlight. "If you don't pass the finish line, you might as well not have run the race."

"Don't talk like that Munch. We'll find another way."

He placed his head back in his hands and together they sat in silence.

She watched his backpack floating in the water. It floated very strangely. It did not bob up and down with the water. Instead, it stayed right where it was while tiny waves splashed up against it. That did not make sense. Unless...

"Munch, what were you carrying in your bag?"

He lifted his head. "Clothing and some cooking pots."

"So, you would say your pack was heavy right?"

"It is very heavy. Why?"

She pointed at his pack that only sunk an inch into the water. "Why is it still floating?"

He turned his head and then stood up abruptly. "I don't believe it."

He looked at her with a massive grin. "It's sitting on the land bridge. It's just right under the water.

He stepped out into the water and walked up to his backpack. He went a few more feet off the shore, but the water never got deep enough to cover the top of his feet completely.

He walked back and picked up his backpack, slung it over one shoulder and looked back at her. "I bet this goes all the way to the castle."

She stepped off the pebbled beach and out into the water. She walked all the way to Munch, each footfall making tiny little splashes, and glanced down at her feet. It looked like she was standing in a shallow puddle. "Do you think the whole lake is only one inch deep?"

Munch ran several feet to her left and stopped abruptly. Then he ran back, passed her and ran a few feet to her right.

He came back to stand next to her. "It looks like we're on a shelf of land. It gets immediately deeper on either side."

He looked at the West Marshal's compound glowing faintly in the moonlight. "Let's see how close we can get to the castle."

They had only been walking for five minutes when Munch stopped short and put a hand up to stop her.

She looked around her, but could not see anything. "What is it?"

He was staring down at the water. She looked to where he directed his attention and saw that the water churned in a small two-foot diameter. Water seemed to rise and fall quickly in this small area. She leaned down next to Munch and spoke quietly, as if somebody on either shore might overhear anything above a whisper. "What is it?"

He peered down into the churning water. "I think it's a vertical tunnel through the bridge down to the rest of the lake. I have noticed them every few dozen steps or so ever since we got into the deepest part of the lake and steered us around them. But this is the first one that seems to be disturbing the water."

A sudden chill crawled up her spine as she looked around.

They were literally standing right in the middle of the lake.

They were completely exposed.

There was no place to hide.

There was nowhere they could run.

If someone decided to come after them right now, there was nothing they could do. She refocused her attention on the churning water. "What do you think is causing that?"

Munch shook his head. "I'm not sure."

"Do you think it might be the snakes?"

He looked over at her. "I haven't seen any."

He stood up. "Let's keep going and just steer clear of these holes."

He took two steps when the hole behind him exploded upward like a geyser. He spun around as a group of snakes shot out with the water, wrapped themselves around him and knocked him to the ground.

Munch screamed as the snakes pulled him back toward the hole.

Dorothy shot forward and grabbed the snake that had wrapped itself around his neck. She tried to pull the snake off him but it held on with an iron grip. As she twisted the snake in her hands, she noticed the entire underbelly was covered in suckers. She looked at the other snakes. They all had the same jagged rows of suckers on their underbellies.

The realization hit her like a ton of bricks.

These were not snakes at all.

These were the arms of an octopus.

She interlocked arms with Munch as she tried to keep the octopus from pulling him into the hole.

He cried out. "I can't feel my legs."

She gripped his clothes with white knuckles and buried her heels in the loose sand of the land bridge. "I've got you!"

The octopus pulled him slowly but steadily through the sand toward the hole. His eyes glazed over and his speech was starting to slur. "Tell my brothers of my heroic deeds."

She twisted her fingers into his clothes tighter, her hands aching from the strain. "I'm not letting you go."

Another water geyser exploded to her left. The snaking tentacles of a second octopus groped the air for her. She kept one eye on the swinging tentacles of the second octopus while fighting with the first for control of Munch.

Munch let go of her arms and now she was the only one keeping the octopus from pulling him into the hole. "Don't give up on me Munch!"

Foam formed around the edges of his lips and he drooled as he spoke. "Run…"

The octopus yanked Munch out of her hands and sucked him down through the hole in an instant.

"Nooooo!"

She bent over the hole on her hands and knees and flailed her arm around in the water.

She had to save him.

Water sloshed up in her face from the hole and she jumped back just as it exploded and tentacles reached out to grab her.

She crab-walked backward quickly on her hands and feet to get out of reach of the tentacles.

Three more geysers exploded around her and tentacles reached for her from every direction. Word had spread quickly that there was food on the land bridge.

She leaped to her feet and ran straight for the castle.

Geysers exploded on either side of her as she ducked to avoid the tentacles that reached for her.

A geyser exploded directly in front of her and she jumped through the air, her foot catching on a twisting tentacle. She landed hard on her side and hydroplaned across the lake's surface for a second before coming to a dead stop in the shallow water.

A tentacle twisted around and touched her boot. She tried to pull her foot back but a second tentacle wrapped itself firmly around her ankle and yanked hard. Her leg twisted with the sudden motion and pain shot up all the way through her spine.

She flopped to her belly and dug her fingers in the sand trying to slow her progress to the hole and the waiting beak of the hungry octopus. It took only moments for the octopus to drag her to the edge of the hole. She took one last breath of air and, just as she went under, a second octopus reached in from above and grabbed her wrists.

She was caught in a tug-of-war between starved cephalopods.

She would be the loser regardless of who won the battle. Her eardrums suddenly compressed painfully and the water pressure increased around her, forcing the last of her air out of her lungs.

The first octopus let go of her legs and disappeared down the tunnel, leaving the second octopus its reward.

The second octopus pulled her quickly up out of the hole.

Sensing air around her, she opened her mouth to suck in the life-sustaining oxygen.

She looked down and saw the lake recede as she continued to rise up in the air. She looked up at the second octopus wrapped around her wrists and instead saw the familiar furry hands of Caleb holding her firmly. He in turn was tied by a rope to an airship that lifted them away from the water.

He smiled down at her. "I've got you."

She looked up at him. "Why did the octopus let go?"

"We dropped a barrel full of gunpowder into the water on a delay fuse. They're sensitive to loud noises."

They were getting closer to the airship as someone pulled the rope back up.

She looked up at Caleb, who looked much thinner with this fir matted down on his body. "Thank you for rescuing me."

Caleb did not smile. "I don't know if I would call this a rescue."

Several hands reached over the edge of the airship gondola loading platform and pulled Caleb and Dorothy into the airship.

Once inside, the door closed and rough hands forced them to kneel on the floor. She saw boots walk in front of them and turn to face them. Dorothy looked up slowly at the owner of the boots until her eyes met those of Amanda.

Standing next to her was a smiling Captain Stiles. "Now, where were we? Ahh, yes. Now I remember."

He raised his rifle over his head and brought the butt of it across Caleb's face.

Chapter 11

Dorothy tripped as the guard shoved her violently into the cell. The clang of the steel bars echoed off the cobblestone walls of the dungeon deep in the underbelly of the West Marshal's castle.

Two other guards tossed the unconscious Caleb into the adjoining cell.

She regained her footing and ran back to the bars, calling out after the guards who were already climbing the stone steps leading up and out of the dungeon.

"I demand to see the West Marshal."

The guards ignored her and disappeared around the bend.

"Do you hear me? My friend could be dying. He needs help."

A voice came to her out of darkness of a neighboring cell on the other side. "There is nothing you could say to convince them to let you out."

She leaned back away from the bars and let her eyes adjust to the darkness. "How do you know?"

A frail looking man, malnourished, with unkempt hair and a matted snow-white beard sat casually against the back wall of his cell. "Because I have tried everything."

"You haven't tried everything."

He frowned. "Why would you say that?"

"You're still here."

He waggled a finger at her. "I didn't ask you why you said that. I asked myself why would you say that."

"Sounds like the same thing to me."

"Ahh, but it is not. They are very different questions. You see I was asking…"

She was not about to get into a philosophical discussion with an ancient prisoner. She cut him off with a wave of her hand. "Hush and let me think."

She circled her cell and inspected every crack and crevice for signs of weakness. She tugged on the bars and pushed at the stone walls.

The old man watched her intently and, after she covered every square inch of her cell a second time, finally spoke. "There is no way out of here."

She turned away from him and looked at the stone steps, the obvious way out of the dungeon. "Why does everyone keep saying that?"

He spoke barely above a whisper. She almost missed it because he had said it so quietly. "Because it's not true."

She spun around and stared at the old man. "What did you just say?"

He smiled and said nothing.

A moan emanated from behind her.

She spun around as Caleb slowly got to his hands and knees.

She ran over and pressed herself against the bars. "Caleb. Are you okay?"

Caleb flopped back into a seated position on the dusty floor and winced when he touched a spot on his forehead. "I think so."

"I thought you were in the southern fields. How did you get caught?"

His deep brown eyes sought her out in the semi-darkness. "There aren't too many hybrids working the fields. I kind of stuck out."

The old man chuckled behind her. She turned around. "What's so funny?"

"Your friend there overstates his situation. There have not been any human animal hybrids in the West in over five years. Just long enough that it should be unexpected for someone like him to be here but not long enough to forget how normal it felt to have them around us all the time."

She glanced back at Caleb and saw that his face registered just as much confusion as she felt from what the old man had just said.

She directed her question at the old man but watched Caleb while she asked it.

"But all the hybrids were killed off a long time ago."

Caleb looked past her toward the man on the other side of her cage. "I'm the last of my kind."

"And who told you that?"

She and Caleb exchanged a quick glance before he responded.

"Mr. Nero."

The old man laughed. "I should've guessed Nero would be involved in such a warping of the truth."

Caleb stood and looked past Dorothy at the old man. "Are you telling me he lied? To me?"

"I don't know exactly what he told you son, but if you think you are the last of your kind, you are greatly mistaken."

"If I am not the last then why have I never seen anyone else like me? And I've been all over OZ."

The man clicked his tongue against the roof of his mouth and stared at Caleb. "The only thing I know is rumors and hints of rumors."

"What kind of rumors?"

"Have you been to the Southern Territories?"

Caleb squinted his eyes. "We both know the answer to that question."

The old man clicked his tongue on the roof of his mouth some more.

"While I was in the Southern Territories, I came across a vacant town. It was not deserted, you see. It was newly built but never lived in. The neighboring towns said it was for the hybrids. I assumed they meant the hybrids already in the Southern Territories. They certainly couldn't mean the hybrids anywhere else in OZ. Nobody gets past the wall or the Southern Marshal's defenses.

"About a year after I was imprisoned down here I heard that every hybrid in the West just disappeared in the middle of the night. There were plenty rumors going around as to what happened to them, but not a single one mentioned the town in the south. Nobody else knew about that but me. I can only assume that is where they went."

Caleb stared at him in silence for a full minute. "You're lying."

"What do I gain from lying to you?"

"I don't know. Some sick satisfaction?"

The old man tilted his head to one side. "A most interesting reason. Now ask yourself this; what did Nero gain from lying to you?"

Caleb opened his mouth and then shut it again.

Dorothy thought of the question as well. Nero gained Caleb as his own personal bodyguard and servant ever since he was a baby. Nero had gained Caleb's entire life in return for lying to him. If he really did lie.

She felt the cold steel of the bars of her cage in her hands and realized they were way off track from what they needed to do. It did not matter who lied to whom if they did not get out of here.

She spun around and marched to the other side of her cage.

"You said something earlier about there being a way out."

The man's face registered shock. "I did?"

"When I asked you why everyone said there was no way out, you replied 'because it's not true'."

The old man smiled. "I thought you caught that."

"Well!?"

"Well what?"

"Do you know a way out of here?"

"Yes I do."

Caleb pressed himself up against the bars of his cage. "Then get us out of here."

The old man studied the both of them for moment and then slipped out a carved chicken bone from between two stones in the wall.

He reached around the front of his cage and inserted the chicken bone into the lock. Within seconds, his door popped open.

He shuffled over and unlocked Dorothy's cage. As the door swung open, her mouth dropped open in surprise. "Who are you?"

The frail old man smiled. "Isn't it obvious? No prison can contain me. I'm the Wizard."

She straightened up in surprise. "We already met the Wizard. Back in his castle."

The old man shuffled toward Caleb's cage. "The wizard you met is only a figurehead. A puppet, if you will, put in place by Nero after he drove me out. Nero is the one who pulls on that puppet's strings."

She stepped out of her cage. "Why are you helping us?"

"Because I'm not really the monster that the world was told this place was built to contain."

Her eyebrows furrowed. "Then who are you?"

The old man turned to face her and bowed slightly. "The name's Jetharo Malonzo, to be precise. I was a spy for Queen Victoria. The best, actually."

He turned back and continued his slow trek to Caleb's cage door. "However, I was betrayed by those closest to me and the enemies of Queen Victoria captured me and imprisoned me. They quickly learned that, given enough time, I could escape. And escape I did, but unfortunately not long enough to make my way back to England. I was recaptured and this time they moved me from prison to prison, not giving me enough time to formulate my escape from any one jail cell."

He jiggled his sharpened chicken bone in the lock to Caleb's cage until he heard a satisfying click.

"When my captors discovered that moving me around so much and keeping it a secret were at odds to each other, they came up with the idea to build a massive prison that could hold me. The part about me being the Wizard because I can escape from any prison is true. The part about me being some indiscriminate street thug is not."

As soon as the cage door swung open, Caleb pounced. He knocked the old man to the ground and growled deep in his chest as he held him down on the floor.

"Why should we believe you?"

Jetharo remained remarkably calm even though he was pinned under a snarling beast. "Easy there, tiger."

Caleb bared his teeth. "I'm a lion."

"Of course you are. My mistake."

Dorothy leaned over Jetharo. "If you really are the Wizard, and you've been able to escape all these years, why are you still here?"

He turned his head to look past Caleb and gave her a warm smile. "I've been waiting for you."

Chapter 12

Dorothy looked around her at the dungeon and at the three open cages. She listened, but did not hear the sounds of guards rushing down the steps to capture them again.

If this was some kind of trick, she still did not know how she was being played.

She looked down at Jetharo who claimed to be the real wizard. Caleb still had him pinned to the ground and growled down at him with each exhale.

She had to know what he was talking about. "What do you mean you've been waiting for me?"

The old man shifted slightly under Caleb's weight. "You are the daughter of Professor Gale, are you not?"

Dorothy's eyes widened as she audibly gasped. This old man had known her father enough to recognize that she was his daughter.

She pushed on Caleb's shoulder. "Let him up."

He barely moved even though she pushed hard on him. He was an immovable object, but she was not an unstoppable force.

He looked up at her. "What do you mean let him up?"

"Let him go. He knows my father."

Instead of letting Jetharo up, Caleb leaned in, pushing the weight of his knee into the old man's chest. "Do you know her father?"

He winced from the increased pressure on his body. "Ben and I were about to escape from OZ when we were captured by the Southern Marshal."

Caleb leaned in even closer, their noses almost touching. He stared silently into Jetharo's eyes before leaning back and getting off him. "He's telling the truth."

Jetharo wheezed with the release of pressure off his chest. The wheezing became a series of violent coughing spasms before he regained his composure and sat up. "Usually big cats are just little cats with a lot of fur. But your friend here is a lot of cat."

Dorothy held out her hand and helped him standup. "Where is my father?"

"Why are you asking me?" He pointed to her chest. "You're the one with the crystal."

Her hand instinctively reached to where her emerald heart necklace hung around her neck. "How do you know about that?"

"I spend a lot of time in the dark. My eyes have adjusted. I saw the faint glow of the necklace through your shirt when the guards brought you in. Your father showed me his crystal and explained they would glow when they got near each other."

"Is my father here?"

"I haven't seen him since the Southern Marshal traded me to the Western Marshal in exchange for medical supplies."

She slipped the necklace out from under her shirt and saw the faint glow. "Then why is it glowing?"

He shrugged. "It's possible that he was also traded to the West Marshal at some point and could be somewhere in the castle. Its faint glow would indicate that he is here."

"I have to find him."

"We will not be able to walk around the castle without being discovered. I can get us out of here, but if you plan to look for your father we cannot escape just yet."

"What you mean?"

"The only one who knows if your father is here or not is the West Marshal. The only way to find out the answer to your question is to ask her."

"And how do you propose I do that?"

Jetharo smiled. "I have a plan if you're not averse to a little risk."

Chapter 13

Caleb half-listened to Jetharo as he outlined a plan to find Dorothy's father and escape from the castle. It did not matter what this old man said. Another plan was already in place.

So far, everything had taken place almost exactly as Nero told him it would. Even when they became separated upon entering the volunteer fields and he thought Nero's plan was shot to hell, they still ended up right where Nero wanted them to be.

Caleb cut Jetharo off mid-sentence. "That'll be enough of that from you."

They both looked at him.

Dorothy had a confused expression on her face. "What's the matter, Caleb?"

He ignored her and called out in a loud voice. "I am ready to see the Queen now."

Three guards turned the corner quickly as if they had been waiting just out of sight. Behind them. Amanda descended the steps at a slower pace.

She smiled at Caleb. "Nero was not kidding when he said you could use Dorothy to get the Wizard to reveal his escape plan."

Dorothy's look of confusion shifted quickly to anger.

Amanda looked at Jetharo. "We will be closing up the weaknesses you discovered in our security. Looks like you'll be staying with us a while longer."

She turned to Caleb. "And you, lion boy…"

He bared his teeth in a sneer. "The name's Caleb."

She waved her hand dismissively. "Whatever. You're to come with me while your girlfriend meets with my mother, the Queen of OZ." She looked over at Dorothy with a smile. "You will do well to remember that while you are in her presence."

Jetharo spoke up. "She is not the Queen of OZ."

Amanda looked at him and bored deeply into his eyes with her own. "She will be by this time tomorrow."

The hint of a smile played at the corners of her mouth. "And I know what her first act as Queen should be." She slid her index finger across her neck in a slicing motion. The hint of a smile broke into a full grin before she spun around and addressed her guards.

"Lock the old man back up and take the East Marshal to see her Queen."

She turned again to Caleb. "This one is coming with me."

As soon as the guards disappeared around the corner with Dorothy, Caleb looked at Amanda. "What are you going to do to her?"

Amanda smiled. "It's not what I'm going to do to her. It's what you're going to do to her."

She led him down the side passageway to a large room lit only by a single candle in the center of the room and filled with glass bottles. "Your master sent a package that will take care of our East Marshal problem. Apparently, only you know how to properly mix the venom so that it will be undetectable by its victim until it is too late."

He smiled. "And that is why Nero sent me to ensure that both the poison was properly formulated and the victim was here."

He started gathering glass vials and bottles before turning to Amanda. "I'm afraid I have to insist that you step outside while I work."

"I'm afraid I can't do that."

"If you will not leave, then I suggest you keep as far back as possible. I will be handling the most deadly substance known to man and if something should happen…" While talking, he fumbled one of the empty glass vials. It slipped from his furry paw and shattered on the floor at his feet.

He looked down at the shattered glass and looked back up at her. "The lion half of my DNA makes me resistant to the venom. This is why I have been the one tasked with handling it. But it still makes me nervous when there's somebody around me who could die because I was clumsy."

Amanda took a step sideways toward the door. "I'll be right outside the door if you need anything."

He smiled. "I will call you as soon as I am done."

She closed the door behind her and he was alone.

He spent the next half hour carefully measuring out the mixture of venom and water. No amount of water could dilute the venom enough to make it harmless. Instead, it created a time delay, a sort of fuse, before the venom became concentrated enough in the body to kill. The more water he added to the mixture, the longer it would take the venom to concentrate.

As he mixed, his thoughts kept returning to the words of the real Wizard down in the dungeon.

If what he said was true, it meant Caleb was not the only hybrid in OZ.

Nero rescued him from death when he was a baby. And Nero reminded him every day that he was the last of his kind. He had even insisted that Caleb call him father.

Why would he do that?

If it was to gain his undying loyalty and trust; it worked.

But now, his trust was shaken.

If there were others like him, why did Nero keep that from him?

When today's task was complete, he would ask Nero to send him on a spy mission to the south to determine their weaknesses in preparation for conquering the Southern Territories.

He would take this time to search for the lost city Jetharo had discovered.

The door latch clanked behind him and ripped him from his thoughts. He turned just as Amanda entered the room. "Are you done yet?"

He picked up a colored ribbon and tied it around the neck of a bottle.

"The bottle with the blue ribbon has the poison in it. The bottle with the red ribbon is just water."

He picked up both bottles and held them out to her. "Make sure you do not confuse the two."

She took the two bottles and inspected them. "Blue is bad. Got it."

Caleb took a deep breath and let it out gradually. "I will return to Nero and let them know it is done."

Amanda frowned. "I would've thought you would want to see this through to the bitter end?"

His eyes shifted to the floor. "I should be getting back. There is still much to do before the next phase."

A wry smile crept onto Amanda's lips. "You've developed feelings for her." She held up the bottle with the blue ribbon tied to its neck. "I trust you've made this no less painful because you like her?"

He lowered his eyes and shook his head.

Her smile warmed. "Good, because you get to watch."

The Adventure Continues...

Sign up for Steve's Book Report (Mailing List) @ SteveDW.com
Know when his next book is released and other trouble he gets into ;-)

Other Books by the Author

A is for Apprentice (Fantasy)

Oliver Twist: Victorian Vampire (Fantasy)

A Tale of Two Cities with Dragons (Fantasy)

Shade Infinity (Science Fiction Thriller)

Peacekeepers X-Alpha Series (Thriller)
        Inherit the Throne
        The Warrior's Code

Steampunk OZ Series (Science Fiction Serial)
        Forgotten Girl
        The Legacy's World
        Emerald Shadow
        The Future's Destiny
        The Dangerous Captive
        Missing Legacy
        Shadow of History
        The Edge of the Hunter

Fugue: The Cure (Science Fiction Short Story)

Stay informed about all the trouble I keep getting into. Subscribe to Steve DeWinter's Book Report (i.e. the mailing list) @ SteveDW.com